For Jamie and Kelly

Text copyright © 2017 by Diane E. Muldrow
Cover photograph copyright © Mary Evans/Classic Stock/H. Armstrong Roberts
All rights reserved.
Published in the United States by Golden Books, an imprint of Random House Children's Books, a division of
Penguin Random House LLC, 1745 Broadway, New York, NY 10019, and in Canada by Penguin Random House
Canada Limited, Toronto. Golden Books, A Golden Book, A Little Golden Book, the G colophon, and the
distinctive gold spine are registered trademarks of Penguin Random House LLC.
The artwork contained in this work was previously published in separate works by Golden Books, New York.
Copyright © 1942–2014 by Penguin Random House LLC. The Poky Little Puppy and The Shy Little Kitten are
trademarks of Penguin Random House LLC.

Copyright page artwork from *Daddies* by Janet Frank, illustrated by Tibor Gergely, copyright © 1953
by Penguin Random House LLC. Title page artwork from *The Bunny Book* by Patsy Scarry, illustrated by
Richard Scarry, copyright © 1955, renewed 1983 by Penguin Random House LLC.

randomhousekids.com
dianemuldrow.com

Library of Congress Control Number: 2014958520

ISBN 978-0-553-53851-9 (trade) — ISBN 978-0-553-53852-6 (lib. bdg.) — ISBN 978-0-553-53853-3 (ebook)
PRINTED IN CHINA
10 9 8 7 6 5 4 3 2

Random House Children's Books supports the First Amendment and celebrates the right to read.

Everything I Need to Know About
to Know About
FAMILY
I Learned From
a Little Golden Book

DIANE MULDROW

A GOLDEN BOOK • NEW YORK

Ah—the perfect family!
Everybody wants one . . .

From *The Happy Family* by Nicole, illustrated by Corinne Malvern, 1955.

**the adorable,
perfectly behaved children**

(who sleep through the night) . . .

From *Prayers for Children*, illustrated by Eloise Wilkin, 1974 edition.

and the perfect house to put them all in.

From *The New House in the Forest* by Lucy Sprague Mitchell, illustrated by Eloise Wilkin, 1946.

From "Rumpelstiltskin," *The Red Little Golden Book of Fairy Tales,*
illustrated by William J. Dugan, 1958.

**So you search until you find
your prince or princess.**

(This may take a while.)

From *The Paper Doll Wedding* by Hilda Miloche and Wilma Kane, 1954.

You get busy planning
the perfect wedding.

Suddenly, you're married!

(It's all a bit of a blur.)

From *The Paper Doll Wedding* by Hilda Miloche and Wilma Kane, 1954.

You get even busier, making your house a home.

Then one day you wake up and think,

From *The House That Jack Built*, illustrated by J. P. Miller, 1954.

"How did this happen?"

From *Bunnies* by Richard Scarry, 1965.

You're not playing house anymore—

From *Come Play House* by Edith Osswald, illustrated by Eloise Wilkin, 1948.

you're in the trenches.

From *Fun with Decals* by Elsa Ruth Nast, illustrated by Corinne Malvern, 1952.

Don't panic!

From *Up in the Attic: A Story ABC* by Hilda K. Williams, illustrated by Corinne Malvern, 1948.

You can do this.

And let's face it . . .

From *Mother Goose*, illustrated by Miss Elliott, 1942.

From *Fun with Decals* by Elsa Ruth Nast, illustrated by Corinne Malvern, 1952.

you've got no choice but to jump in!

From *When You Were a Baby* by Rita Eng, illustrated by Corinne Malvern, 1949.

**Just make sure to never
run out of diapers,**

hang on to your couple time,

From *Gaston and Josephine* by Georges Duplaix, illustrated by Feodor Rojankovsky, 1949.

and let the kids help!

From *Baby's House* by Gelolo McHugh, illustrated by Mary Blair, 1950.

Family life does bring some challenges.

From *Naughty Bunny* by Richard Scarry, 1959.

You may have the occasional moment when you wonder what you were thinking when you chose your particular spouse.

(That's okay.)

From "Beauty and the Beast," *The Blue Book of Fairy Tales*, illustrated by Gordon Laite, 1959.

You try so hard to teach your kids how to behave.

From *The Golden Animal ABC*, illustrated by Garth Williams, 1954.

Sometimes you wonder if they hear *anything* you say!

From *Naughty Bunny* by Richard Scarry, 1959.

It's a good thing they're so cute.

From *Baby's House* by Gelolo McHugh, illustrated by Mary Blair, 1950.

(Especially when they're finally asleep.)

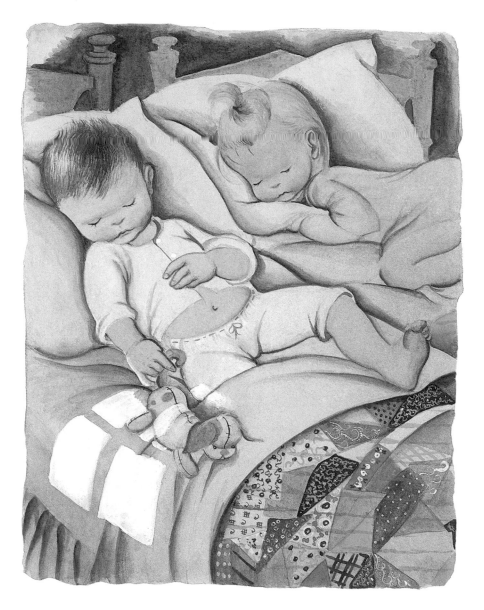

From *The New House in the Forest* by Lucy Sprague Mitchell, illustrated by Eloise Wilkin, 1946.

There's no "perfect family," despite what people may want you to think.

From *The Happy Family* by Nicole, illustrated by Gertrude Elliott, 1947.

And families don't have to be all-of-a-kind.

From *The Kitten Who Thought He Was a Mouse* by Miriam Norton, illustrated by Garth Williams, 1951.

Family life is made of moments big

From *The New Baby* by Ruth and Harold Shane, illustrated by Eloise Wilkin, 1948.

and small,

From *Mister Dog* by Margaret Wise Brown, illustrated by Garth Williams, 1952.

moments that bind us over time . . .

From *Baby Sister* by Dorothea M. Sachs, illustrated by Joy Friedman, 1986.

moments that are happy times,

From *Good Night, Little Bear* by Patsy Scarry, illustrated by Richard Scarry, 1961.

and first times,

From *A Day at the Seashore* by Kathryn and Byron Jackson, illustrated by Corinne Malvern, 1951.

and day-to-day times . . .

From *Doctor Dan the Bandage Man* by Helen Gaspard, illustrated by Corinne Malvern, 1950.

hours spent together over meals,

From *Ukelele and Her New Doll* by Clara Louise Grant, illustrated by Campbell Grant, 1951.

From *The Fuzzy Duckling* by Jane Werner Watson, illustrated by Alice and Martin Provensen, 1949.

times that give us a sense of belonging,

when we feel safe

From *My Little Golden Book About God*
by Jane Werner Watson,
illustrated by Eloise Wilkin, 1956.

and loved.

From "The Cold Little Squirrel," *The Animals' Merry Christmas* by Kathryn Jackson,
illustrated by Richard Scarry, 1958.

Our siblings are our first playmates, our original co-conspirators, the ones who "knew us when."

From *The Twins* by Ruth and Harold Shane, illustrated by Eloise Wilkin, 1955.

**Grandparents and uncles and aunts
give us a fuller sense of ourselves
and who we can be.**

From *The Bunny Book* by Patsy Scarry, illustrated by Richard Scarry, 1955.

We may not always feel that our family understands us. . . .

From *When I Grow Up* by Kay and Harry Mace, illustrated by Corinne Malvern, 1950.

Luckily, our pets do!

We hope and dream
for our children. . . .

From "Cradle Song," *The New Golden Song Book*, A Giant Golden Book, illustrated by Mary Blair, 1955.

**We want so much for them to have
a magical childhood.**

From *The Little Golden Holiday Book* by Marion Conger, illustrated by Eloise Wilkin, 1951.

Sometimes we wonder if we can measure up to be the parents we should be.

One of the best things about being a parent is getting to be a kid again!

Both pages: From *Animal Daddies and My Daddy* by Barbara Shook Hazen,
illustrated by Ilse-Margret Vogel, 1968.

Oh, the girls,

From *Come Play House* by Edith Osswald, illustrated by Eloise Wilkin, 1948.

the boys!

From *Jack's Adventure* by Edith Thacher Hurd, illustrated by J. P. Miller, 1958.

The tantrums!

From *Good Little, Bad Little Girl* by Esther Wilkin, illustrated by Eloise Wilkin, 1965.

The noise!

From *Little Boy with a Big Horn* by Jack Bechdolt, illustrated by Aurelius Battaglia, 1950.

The chubby cheeks . . .

From *Baby's Christmas* by Esther Wilkin, illustrated by Eloise Wilkin, 1959.

the clamor for sweets!

From "The Three Little Kittens," *Three Bedtime Stories*, illustrated by Garth Williams, 1958.

Every family knows that first day of kindergarten,

From *We Like Kindergarten* by Clara Cassidy, illustrated by Eloise Wilkin, 1965.

the sound of a giggly baby,

and all those baby things!

Both pages: From *When You Were a Baby* by Rita Eng, illustrated by Corinne Malvern, 1949.

Remember those long car trips

From *Cars and Trucks* by Richard Scarry, 1959.

and the vacation
when it rained every day?

From *Fun with Decals* by Elsa Ruth Nast, illustrated by Corinne Malvern, 1952.

We all make our own happy traditions
that we anticipate each year

From *The Little Golden Holiday Book* by Marion Conger, illustrated by Eloise Wilkin, 1951.

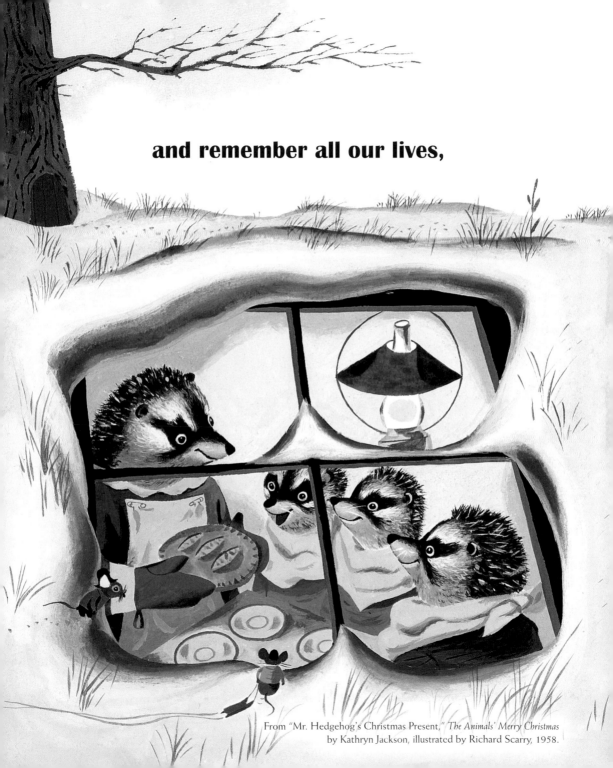

and remember all our lives,

From "Mr. Hedgehog's Christmas Present," *The Animals' Merry Christmas*
by Kathryn Jackson, illustrated by Richard Scarry, 1958.

**traditions that bring us together
from across the miles.**

From "The Country Mouse and the City Mouse," *Three Aesop Fables,* told by Patricia Scarry,
illustrated by Richard Scarry, 1961.

**Days and nights turn into months
and years together . . .**

From *Guess Who Lives Here* by Louise Woodcock, illustrated by Eloise Wilkin, 1949.

**and soon the kids are heading out
on their own.**

From *Animal Friends* by Jane Werner Watson, illustrated by Garth Williams, 1953.

**Where does
the time go?**

From *The Little Golden Holiday Book* by Marion Conger, illustrated by Eloise Wilkin, 1951.

Children don't stay little forever . . .

so let's enjoy reading their favorite book
for the millionth time

From *Daddies* by Janet Frank, illustrated by Tibor Gergely, 1953.

and let kids
be kids.

From "The Wolf and the Kids," *The Three Billy Goats Gruff and The Wolf and the Kids,*
illustrated by Richard Scarry, 1953.

Let's stick together

From *The Three Bears*, illustrated by Feodor Rojankovsky, 1948.

in times of plenty,

From "The Country Mouse and the City Mouse," *Three Aesop Fables*, told by Patricia Scarry, illustrated by Richard Scarry, 1961.

and when the wolf is at the door.

From "The Three Little Pigs," *Three Bedtime Stories,* illustrated by Garth Williams, 1958.

Every day's a fresh start.

From *A Day at the Seashore* by Kathryn and Byron Jackson, illustrated by Corinne Malvern, 1951.

**And it all begins
with our love,
and our hope**

From *The Giant Golden Book of Elves and Fairies*, selected by Jane Werner Watson,
illustrated by Garth Williams, 1951.

for the ones we call family.

From *The Shy Little Kitten* by Cathleen Schurr, illustrated by Gustaf Tenggren, 1946.